To my wife, Christine, who made Christmas fun again

First edition 2010

Library of Congress Cataloging-in-Publication Data

Light, Steve.
The Christmas giant / Steve Light.—1st ed.
p. cm.
Summary: When two best friends, a giant and an elf, grow Christmastown's holiday tree, disaster strikes.
ISBN 978-0-7636-4692-9
[1. Giants—Fiction. 2. Elves—Fiction. 3. Best friends—Fiction. 4. Friendship—Fiction.
5. Christmas trees—Fiction. 6. Christmas—Fiction.] I. Title.
PZ7.L6256Ch 2010
[E]—dc22 2009049101

10 11 12 13 14 15 SCP 10 9 8 7 6 5 4 3 2 1

Printed in Humen, Dongguan, China

This book was typeset in Dickens.
The illustrations were done in pen and ink using a Pelikan M805 and Mont Blanc 149 fountain pen.
They were then colored using Rembrandt and Winsor and Newton soft pastels.

Candlewick Press
99 Dover Street
Somerville, Massachusetts 02144

visit us at www.candlewick.com

The Christmas Giant

STEVE LIGHT

CANDLEWICK PRESS

Humphrey and Leetree are great friends.

Humphrey is a giant. Leetree is an elf. They live at the North Pole.

They make the wrapping paper for all Santa's gifts.

They love making wrapping paper.

Just before Christmas, they deliver the paper to Santa's Workshop.

But when their work is done for the year,
Humphrey and Leetree are sad.

One year Santa gives Humphrey and Leetree a special assignment:
to grow the holiday tree for Christmastown.

They are so excited! Leetree plants the small seed.

Humphrey carries the big can of water.

Humphrey moves the big rock.

Leetree pulls the small weeds.

Leetree trims the low branches.

Humphrey trims the high branches.

Finally the tree is ready.

They set off.

Soon they are very tired. They stop to rest.

“Oh, no!” says Humphrey.

Humphrey and Leetree look

and look

and look, but they cannot find the tree.

They try to figure out what to do.

Then Humphrey gets a small idea, and Leetree makes a big plan.

They set off again.

Leetree unties the bow. Humphrey opens the box.

ooooOhh!

Aaaaah!

It is the best Christmas tree anyone has ever seen—

especially Santa.

Humphrey gives Leetree a little squeeze.
Leetree gives Humphrey a big hug.

Merry Christmas!